Cossey

HARVEY'S HIDEOUT

BY RUSSELL HOBAN

PICTURES BY LILLIAN HOBAN

Four Winds Press   New York

Library of Congress Cataloging in Publication Data

Hoban, Russell.
  Harvey's hideout.

  SUMMARY: Harvey thinks his big sister is mean
and rotten; she thinks he is stupid and no-good. As
a result, they both spend some lonely hours refusing
to play with each other.
  [1. Brothers and sisters—Fiction. 2. Muskrats—Fic-
tion] I. Hoban, Lillian. II. Title.
PZ7.H637Har 1980   [E]   80-15292
ISBN 0-590-07767-8

Published by Four Winds Press
A division of Scholastic Magazines, Inc., New York, N.Y.
Text copyright © 1969 by Russell Hoban
Illustrations copyright © 1969 by Lillian Hoban
Printed in the United States of America
Library of Congress Catalog Card Number: 80-15292
1 2 3 4 5 84 83 82 81 80

For big sisters and little brothers
in dens, burrows, and houses everywhere

It was a quiet summer afternoon,
and Harvey Muskrat was building a raft in the backyard.
He was hammering hard when his big sister Mildred
stuck her head out of the window.
"Harvey, you stop that hammering!" said Mildred.
"I can't," said Harvey. "I'm building a raft."

"Build it someplace else," said Mildred.
"I'm writing a poem."
"I can't," said Harvey.
"This is where the hammer and nails
and all my planks and logs are. Why don't you
go someplace else to write your poem?"
"It's my house as much as it is yours," said Mildred.

"And it's my backyard as much as it is yours,"
said Harvey.
"You are being selfish and inconsiderate,"
said Mildred, "and I'm telling."
"Go ahead and tell," said Harvey,
and he went on hammering until
his mother came out on the back porch.

"Harvey," said Mother, "that is a terrible racket
to make so close to the house. You really ought to
do your hammering somewhere else."
"So, ha ha ha," said Mildred,
and she stuck out her tongue at Harvey.
Harvey stuck out his tongue back at Mildred.
Then he piled his tools on his planks and logs
and swam with them to the other side of the pond
to finish his hammering.

When the raft was finished, Harvey poled it
back across the pond and went fishing on the raft
where Mildred could see him from her window.
When Mildred saw Harvey,
she called, "Can I have a ride on the raft?"

"No," said Harvey, "because this is not the house
and it is not the backyard and no part of it is yours.
It is my raft and nobody else's. So, ha ha ha."
"That is just what I would expect
from a selfish, inconsiderate, stupid, no-good
little brother like you," said Mildred.

"That is because you are a loudmouth, bossy,
mean and rotten big sister," said Harvey
as Mother came out on the back porch again.
"You will both have to stop that right now,"
said Mother, "and your father
is going to hear about it when he comes home."

When Father came rowing home in his boat
and opened the front door he heard about it.
"Mildred," said Father, "it is true
that Harvey is selfish and inconsiderate,
but he is not stupid and no-good,
and you are not allowed to call him that."
"What about what he called me?" said Mildred.
"Mildred is loudmouthed and bossy," said Father to Harvey,
"but she is not mean and rotten, and after supper
both of you will have sentences to write."
So after supper Harvey had to write
I will not call Mildred mean and rotten
five hundred times.
Mildred had to write
I will not call Harvey stupid and no-good
five hundred times.

"Well," said Mildred to Harvey
when they had finished their sentences
and were standing in the hallway outside their rooms,
"you see how much trouble we got into,
and that is what happens with selfish, inconsiderate,
stupid, no-good little brothers."
"Only when they have loudmouth, bossy,
mean and rotten big sisters," said Harvey.

Both of them spoke very quietly
so that Mother and Father would not hear them.
"All right," said Mildred. "You will be sorry,
because I know something you don't know."
"What?" said Harvey.
"There is a big party that I am going to tomorrow,"
said Mildred, "and little brothers are not invited."
"I don't care," said Harvey,
"because I know something you don't know."
"What?" said Mildred.
"There is a secret club that I belong to
that meets in a secret place," said Harvey,
"and big sisters are not allowed to be members."
"Well, I don't care," said Mildred,
"because anything that you are a member of
I would not want to belong to."

"And any party that you go to," said Harvey,
"I would not want to be invited to."
Then Mildred and Harvey stuck their tongues out
at each other, slammed the doors of their rooms quietly,
and went to bed.

The next day Mildred tried on several party dresses
until she decided which one to wear.
Then she folded up the dress very small,
wrapped it in plastic sandwich wrap to keep it dry,
and swam off across the pond
with her party dress in her mouth.
Harvey watched her come out on the far bank
and go into the woods.
He waited until Mildred was out of sight,
and then he poled his raft across the pond
and he went into the woods, too.

That evening after supper Mildred said to Harvey,
"That was a wonderful party this afternoon."
"We had a really good meeting at the secret club,"
said Harvey.
"There were all kinds of refreshments," said Mildred.
"Cake and soda and ice cream."
"We had a cookout," said Harvey,
"with all kinds of good things.
We had hot dogs and baked beans and cole slaw
and potato chips and root beer
and toasted marshmallows afterwards.
It was a lot of fun."
"Who was at the secret club meeting?" said Mildred.
"Different kids," said Harvey. "Nobody you know.
Who was at the party?"
"Nobody you know," said Mildred.

"They were all very *nice,* and *polite,*
and *considerate,* and there were no little brothers at all,
and there will be another party tomorrow."
"There is another secret club meeting tomorrow, too,"
said Harvey, "and we will have a lot of fun again
with no big sisters there."

The next day Mildred came out of the house
with a bundle that she had made
by tying some things up in her yellow slicker.
When she was ready to swim across the pond with it
she found Harvey waiting at the dock with his raft.

On the raft was a bundle that Harvey had made
by wrapping up some things in his poncho.
"You can have a ride across the pond with me
if you want," said Harvey. "I'm going that way anyhow."
"All right," said Mildred, "but no following
me to the party, and no looking
at what is in my bundle."
"All right," said Harvey, "and no looking
at my stuff and no following me."
Harvey poled the raft across to the other side of the pond,
and Mildred started off on the path through the woods.

Harvey waited until she was just out of sight,
and then he followed her.
He was coming around a bend in the path
when Mildred jumped out from behind a bush.
"I told you no following," she said.
"I'm not following," said Harvey. "I was just looking
for something I lost around here yesterday,
but I can look for it later, when you're gone."

Mildred went off down the path again
and Harvey turned around and slowly went the other way.
He went back to the raft
and picked up his poncho bundle.
Then he went into the woods
and followed a trail to a den he had dug
in the ground near the banks of the pond.

There was a tunnel to the underground den,
and the opening of the tunnel
was covered up with brush so that nobody could find it.
In the floor of the den was a hole lined with stones
for building a fire in, and in the ceiling
was a hole for letting the smoke out.
On one of the walls was a calendar from the milkman
with a picture of a muskrat baby on it.
On another wall was a drawing of an Indian
that Harvey had made.
Out of the poncho Harvey took
an egg and two strips of bacon,
a small frying pan that his mother did not use anymore,
an empty milk bottle,
and a stack of secondhand comic books
he had traded for at school.
Harvey piled the comic books in a corner of the den.

Then he took the milk bottle down to the pond,
filled it with water and put some wild flowers in it.
Harvey stood the milk bottle of flowers
on the floor of the den in the place
where it looked best, under the calendar.
Then he fried the egg and bacon and had his lunch.

Then he dug a getaway tunnel down to the pond,
so that the secret club would have a secret exit.
Then he sat down and sighed
and read his old comic books, because
there was nobody for him to talk to
and nobody for him to play with.
His best friend, Howard Woodchuck, was at camp,
and his next best friends, the Chipmunk children,
had gone away with their parents for the summer.

The Beaver children were all too big to be his friends,
and they made fun of him because
he was not good at cutting down trees.
The Opossum children always laughed at him
because he could not swing from a branch by his tail.
The Rabbit children were all too fast
for him to run around with.
His mother had told him not to
play with the Raccoon children because
they knocked over garbage cans,
and his father had warned him
not to get mixed up with the Weasels.
So there was nobody in the secret club but Harvey,
and that is why there was nobody
in the secret clubhouse but Harvey.
Harvey thought about Mildred
and the good time she was having at her party.
She was probably having cake and ice cream,
and the girls would be wearing pretty dresses
and they would be playing games.

Harvey wished that little brothers
were allowed to go to the party, but he decided
that he would never tell that to Mildred,
and he would never tell her that he was
the only member of the secret club.
Harvey thought about it for a long time,
and after a while he began to cry a little
and he did not want to read his comic books anymore.

So he decided to do some more digging in the den
to make it a better shape and a little bit bigger.
Harvey took down the calendar and the Indian picture
and he moved the milk bottle of flowers
and he began to dig.
Harvey dug and carried out dirt until he was tired,
and then he sat down to rest.
While he was resting he thought he heard
something under the ground close by.
Harvey leaned against the wall where he had been digging
so that he could listen better.
When he leaned against the wall
part of it crumbled away, and there was a little hole
that Harvey could hear a voice coming out of.
The voice said, "Have another cup of tea, Lucinda.
Have some cake."

Harvey knew who Lucinda was,
and he knew whose voice that was.
He put his eye to the hole, and he saw
that on the other side of the hole
was another underground den right next to his.

And inside that den was his big sister Mildred
and her old doll, Lucinda, who had one leg
and her tail missing.
They were both wearing party dresses,
and they were having a tea party.
Mildred had spread a cloth on the ground
and she had brought her tea set.
She had real vanilla wafers for cake,
but she had only pretend tea,
and she had no pictures on the walls
and no flowers and no comic books.
When Mildred looked up and saw Harvey
she was very angry. "That is *sneaking,*" she said,
"and that is *spying,* and it is *nasty,*
and when we get home I'm telling."
"I *wasn't* sneaking and spying," said Harvey.

"I didn't know you had a secret place next to mine.
I thought you really went to parties."
"That is just plain stupid of you to think that,"
said Mildred, "when you know that my best friend,
Lavinia Otter, is away for the summer,
and so is my other friend, Rachel Squirrel,
and the Beaver kids are all too big
for either of us to play with
and the Opossums are not good for anything

but swinging by their tails and the Rabbits
are too fast to run around with and the Raccoons
knock over garbage cans and we are not allowed
to get mixed up with the Weasels.
So I would like to know just who you think there is
for me to have a party with, Mister Nasty Little Brother."
Then Harvey began to cry,
and he rubbed his eye with his paw
and got dirt in his eye and cried harder.

Then he threw some dirt at Mildred
and made her party dress dirty, and she began to cry.

"You are so *mean!*" said Harvey.
"And I wasn't sneaking and spying
and I was going to give you half of my comic books
and a calendar for your wall if you wanted one
and I have a cooking hole and I thought
next time we could have a real cookout party,
but you are too *mean*."

Mildred stopped crying.

"How come?" she said to Harvey.

"How come what?" said Harvey.

"How come you were going to give me comic books
and a calendar and you wanted to have a cookout
and all that?" said Mildred.

"Because I am lonesome," said Harvey,
"and there is nobody but you to play with,
and I was going to be nice."
"Would you make fun of my poems and my tea parties?"
said Mildred. "Would you laugh when I talk to Lucinda?"

"No," said Harvey. "I wouldn't. Would you say
mean things about the pictures I draw and would you
tell me that I do everything wrong when I cook?"
"No," said Mildred. "I wouldn't.
"Would you like to have a cup of tea with me and Lucinda?"
"All right," said Harvey. "If we make this hole bigger
it can be a doorway between your place and my place."
"And we can visit back and forth," said Mildred.
So Harvey and Mildred made the hole into a doorway,
and they ate vanilla wafers
and drank pretend tea with Lucinda.
And the next time they came there
the secret club had two members
and Lucinda had two friends to talk to
at the tea party next door.